The Hat

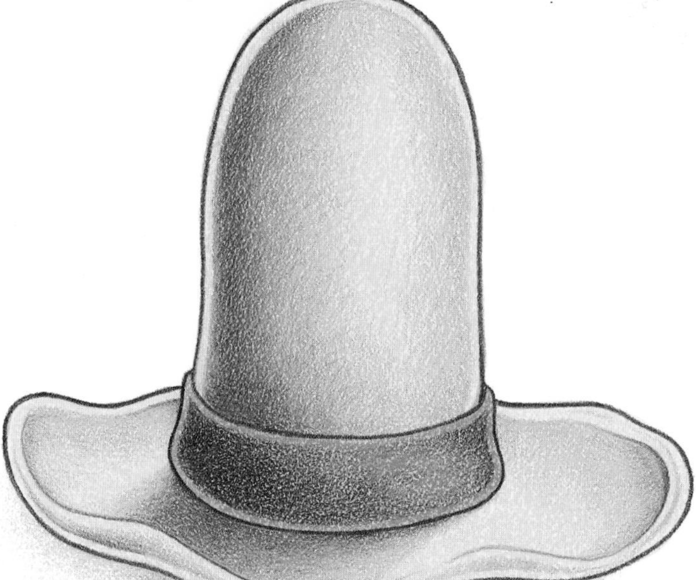

Written by Emily Miller
Illustrated by Gregg Valley

Scott Foresman

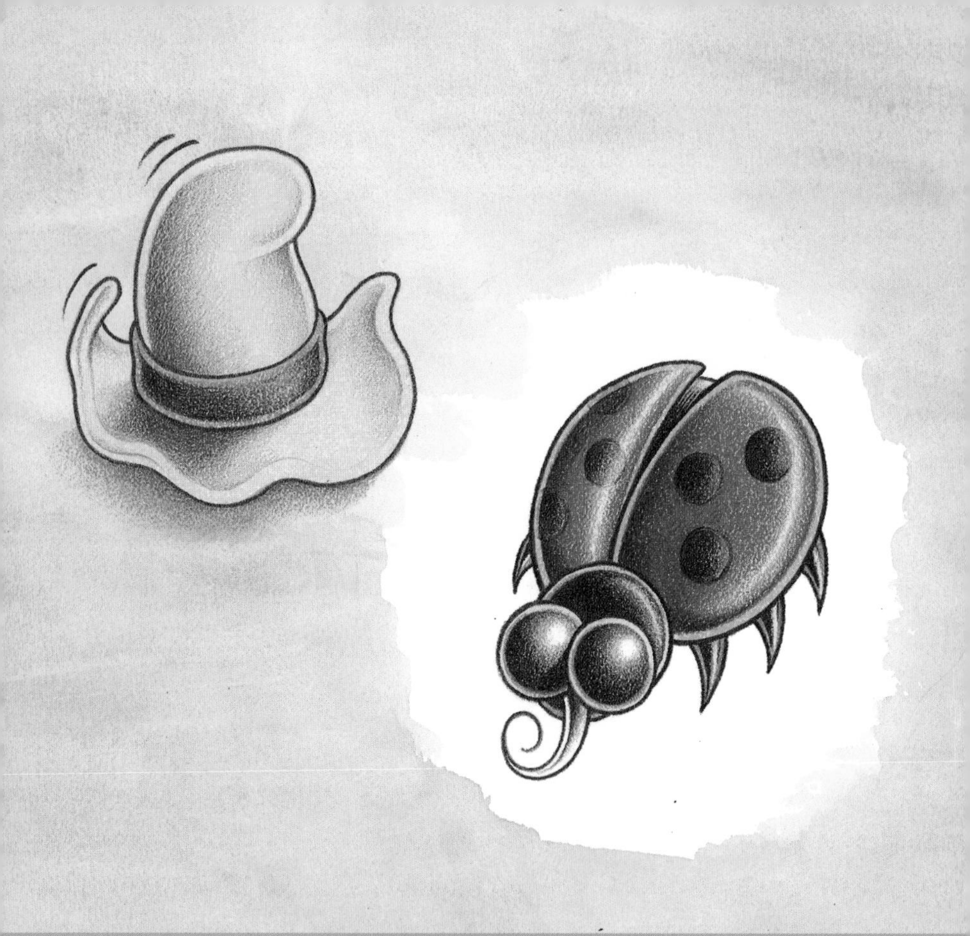

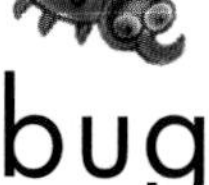

bug

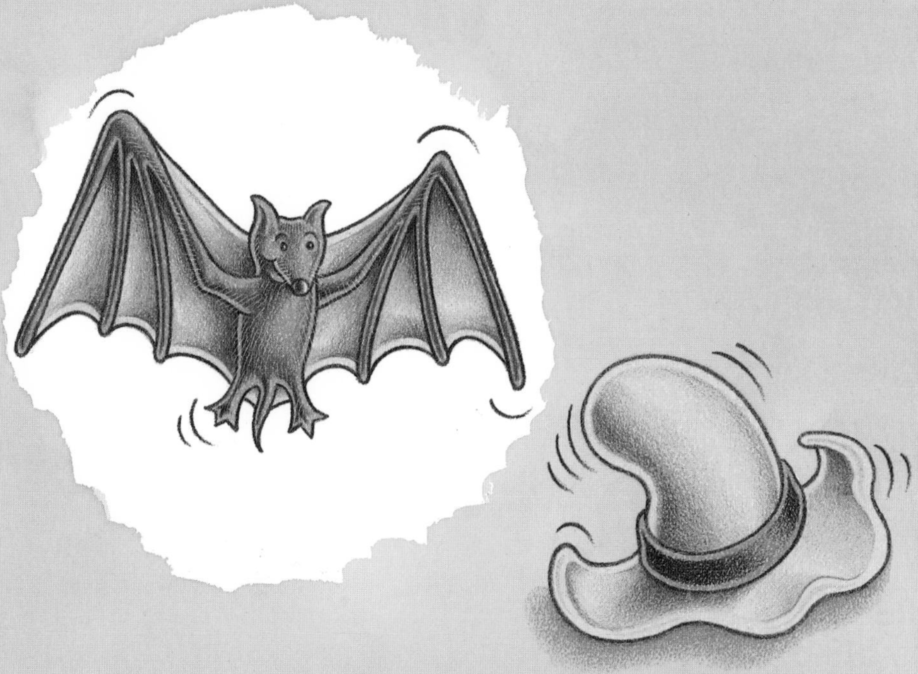

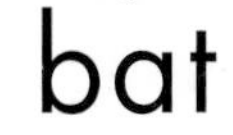

bat

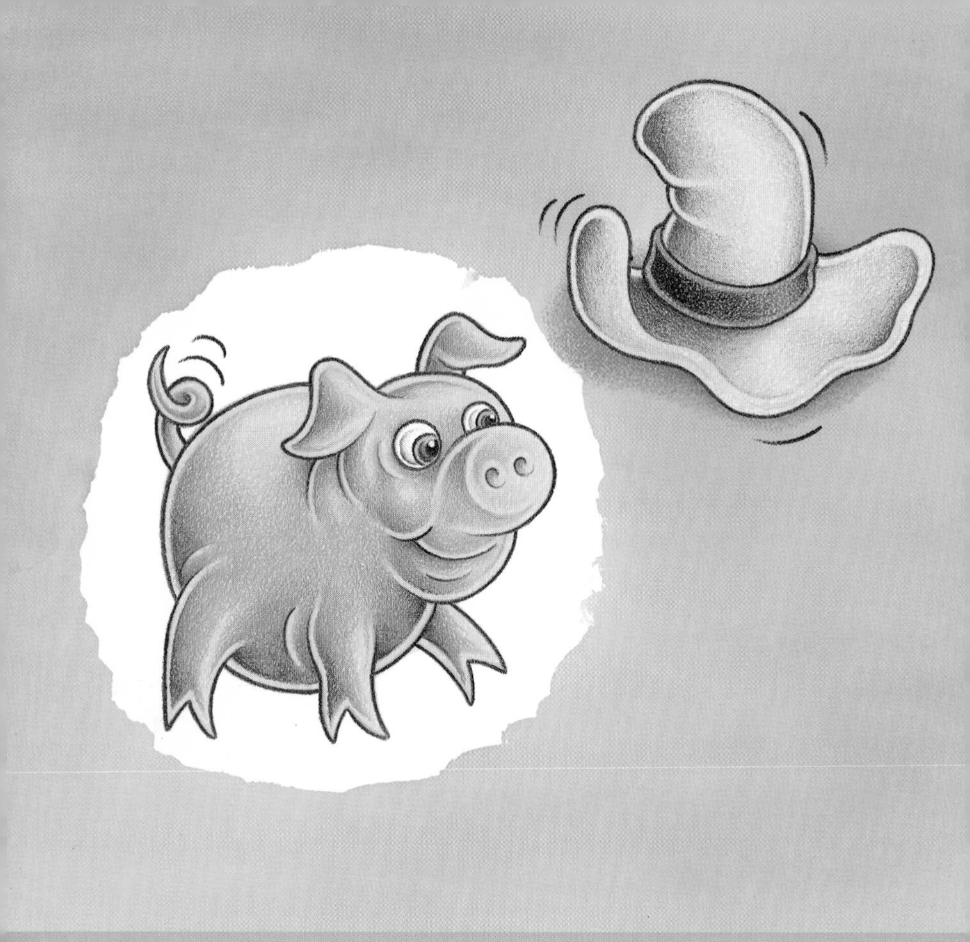

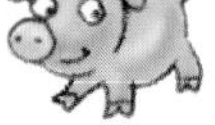

pig

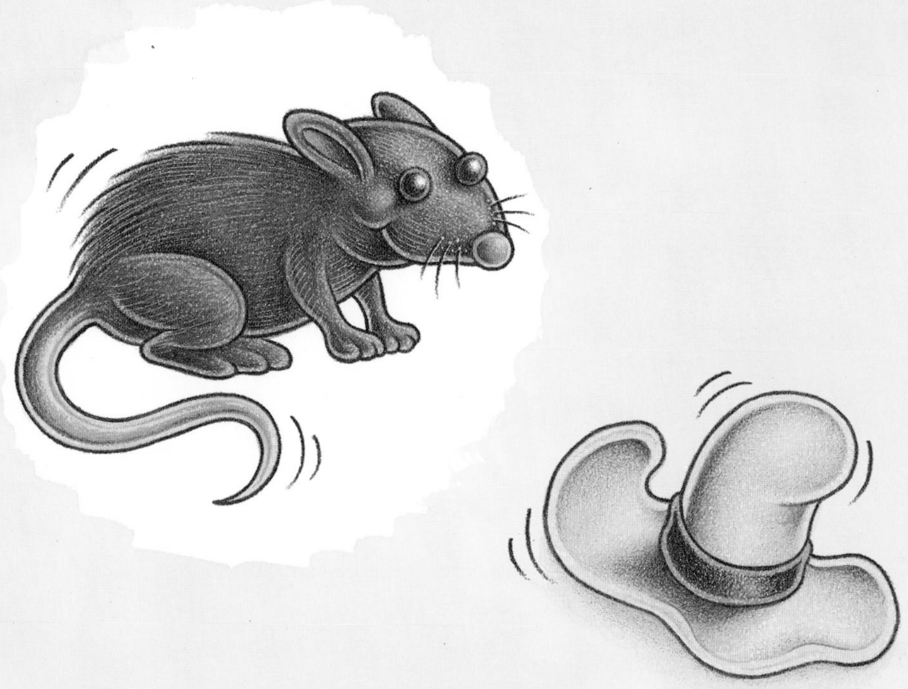

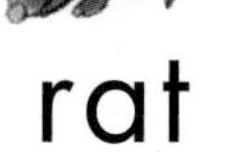

rat

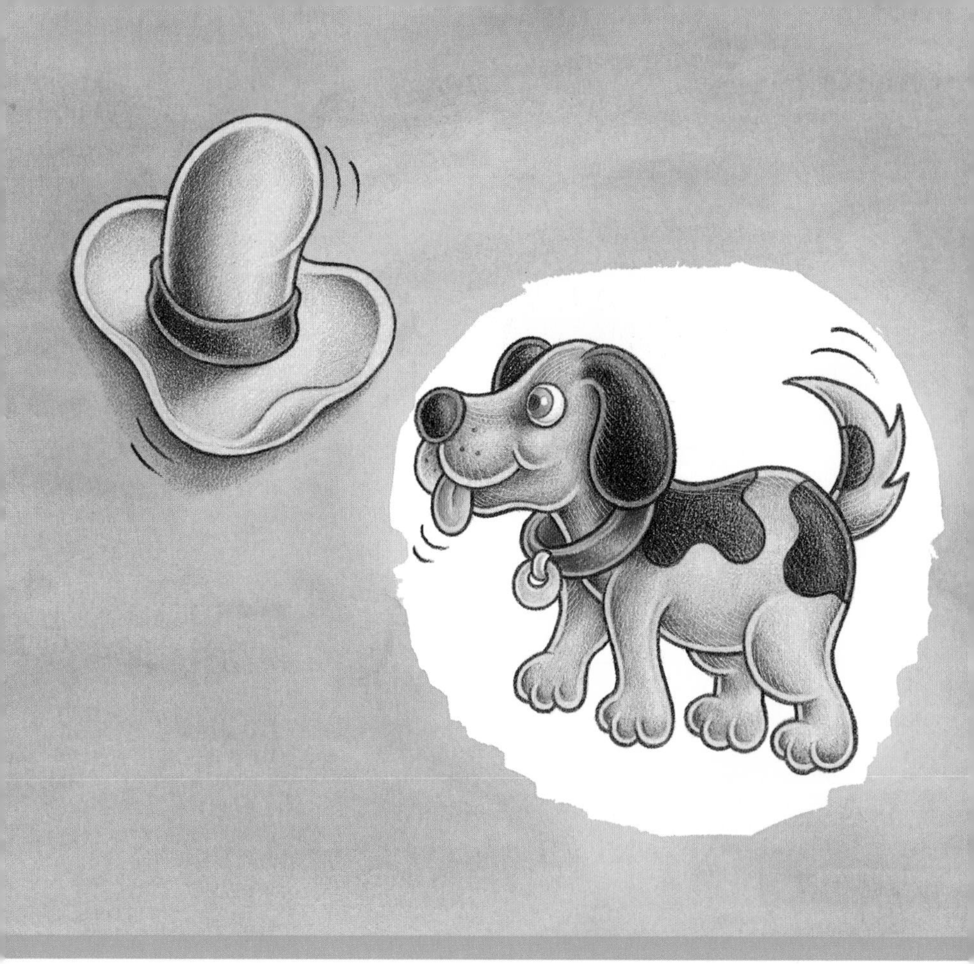

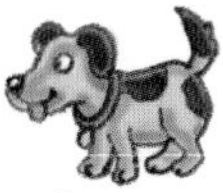

dog

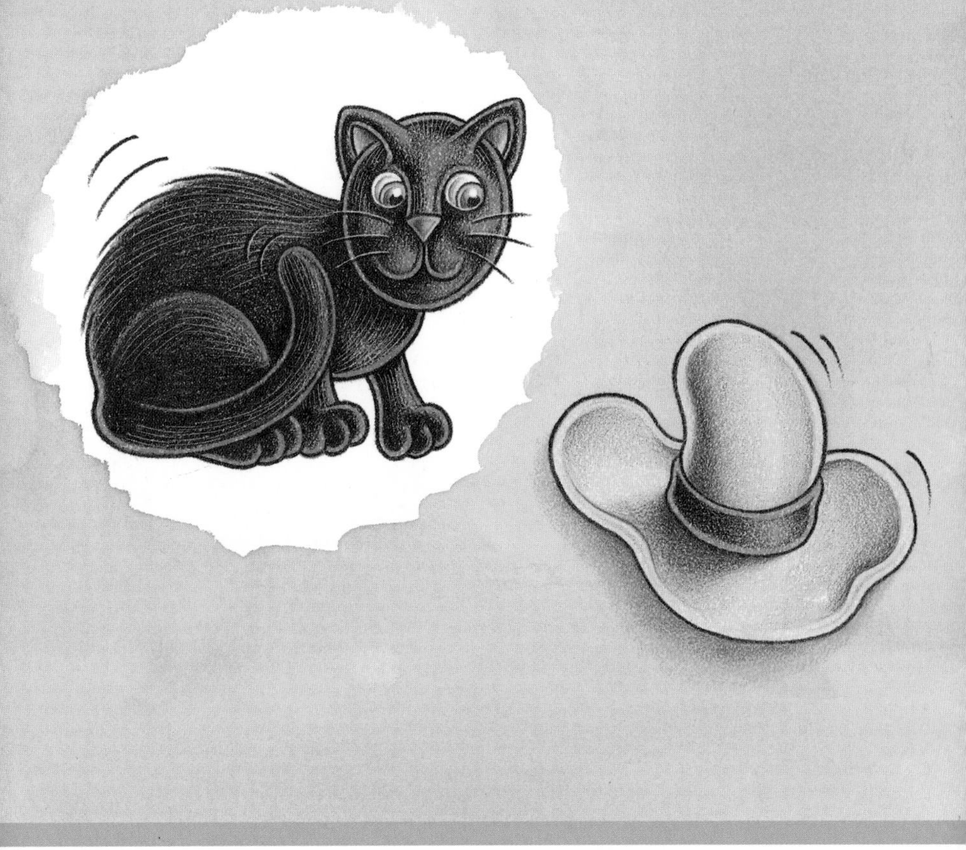

cat

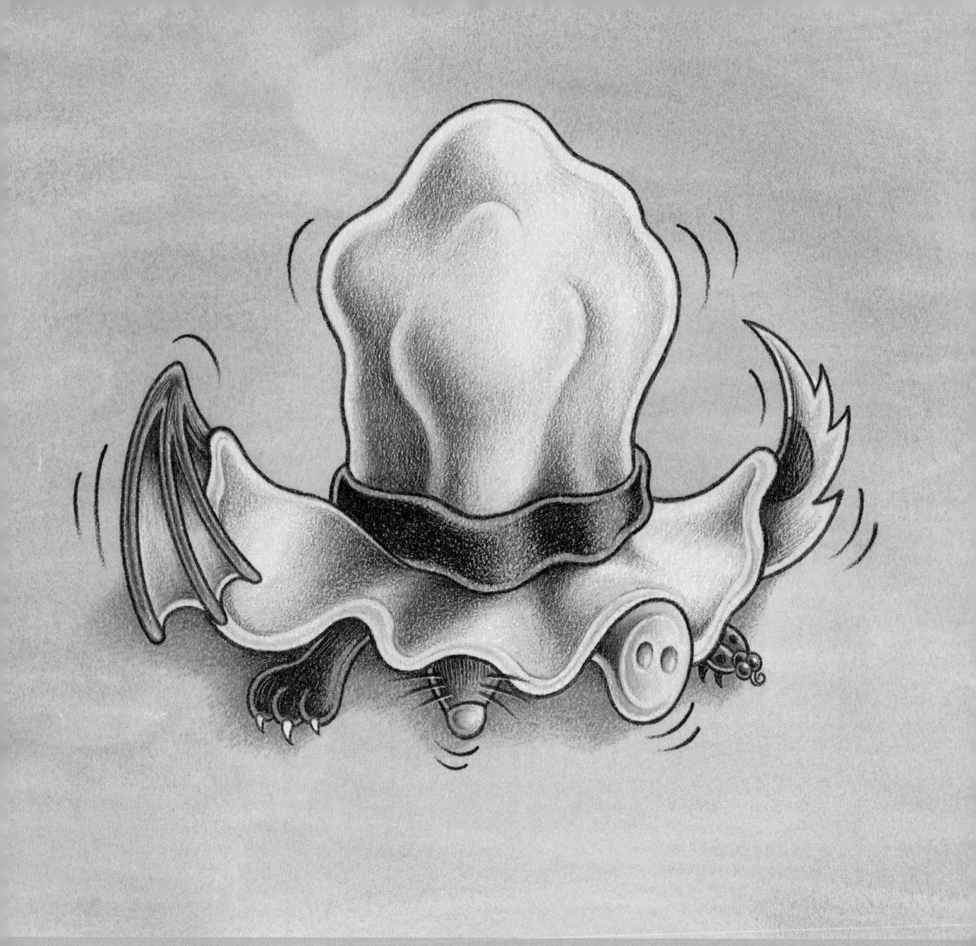

The hat!